The Best Bed for Me

GAIA CORNWALL

WALKER BOOKS

AND SUBSIDIARIES

LONDON · BOSTON · SYDNEY · AUCKLAND

"Time for bed, Sweet Pea," my mama says.
"Where's my tree?"
"Tree?"

"I want to sleep high up in a tree like the koalas!"

"OK, goodnight, little koala," my mama says.

"Or maybe I'll sleep like …

"a sea otter! We could hold hands all night long."

"You do love to snuggle, little otter. Now time for—"

"You know who else loves to snuggle, Mama?

"Piglets! They curl up in the mud."

"Piglet," my mama says,
"you must be tired. Let's—"
"It might be too muddy. Maybe I'll sleep cuddled down like ...

"a puffin! A burrow will be nice and dry."

"Thank goodness I have a burrow right here for you!"

"But I think it's too small. I need to stretch out ...

"like a whale in the ocean!
They keep swimming even when they sleep!"

"Well, you are a good swimmer.

How 'bout you float right under these blankets,
my whale," says my mama.

"But I don't know if I can swim all night long.

Maybe I could sleep upside down like …

"a bat! They hold on with their feet
and hang down from branches."

"My little bat, it's time to calm our bodies down."

"Maybe it would be relaxing to sleep standing up!
Like an …

"emperor penguin! Oh, they're my favourite! They don't even let their toes touch the ground."

"Little penguin, do you know how my favourite sleeps?"
"What is your favourite, Mama?"

"You. You're my favourite."

"Well, I sleep in this big-kid bed, with a soft pillow
and a fluffy blanket. It's the best bed for me."

"Goodnight, Sweet Pea."
"Goodnight, Mama."
"Sweet dreams."

I created the bulk of this book during a year of COVID upheaval. And so it seems especially fitting that I dedicate it, with my whole heart, to parents and caregivers everywhere, especially at bedtime when everyone *is exhausted. May we channel Mama's patience and all have meltdown-free nights forevermore. We certainly deserve them.*

First published in the UK 2022 by Walker Books Ltd, 87 Vauxhall Walk, London SE11 5HJ · © 2022 Gaia Cornwall · The right of Gaia Cornwall to be identified as author and illustrator of this work has been asserted by her in accordance with the Copyright, Designs and Patents Act 1988 This book has been typeset in Mrs. Eaves · Printed in Italy ·
· British Library Cataloguing in Publication Data: a catalogue record for this book is available from the British Library · ISBN 978-1-5295-0636-5 · 10 9 8 7 6 5 4 3 2 1